Hello Kitty

and friends

The Big Race

·A HELLO KITTY ADVENTURE·

Hello Kitty

and friends

The Big Race

·A HELLO KITTY ADVENTURE·

HarperCollins *Children's Books*

MEET

Hello Kitty
and friends

Hello Kitty

Mimmy

Tammy

Mama

Papa

Grandpa

Grandma

Fifi

Dear Daniel

With special thanks to
Linda Chapman and Michelle Misra

First published in Great Britain by HarperCollins *Children's Books* in 2014

www.harpercollins.co.uk
1 3 5 7 9 10 8 6 4 2
ISBN: 978-000-751610-0

Printed and bound in England by Clays Ltd, St Ives plc.

MIX
Paper from
responsible sources
FSC™ C007454

FSC™ is a non-profit international organisation established to promote
the responsible management of the world's forests. Products carrying the
FSC label are independently certified to assure consumers that they come
from forests that are managed to meet the social, economic and
ecological needs of present and future generations,
and other controlled sources.

Find out more about HarperCollins and the environment at
www.harpercollins.co.uk/green

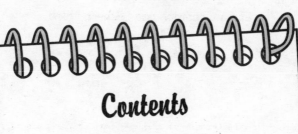

Contents

Exciting News!

Hello Kitty put her books away and started

to draw a doodle as the rest of the class

finished packing up. She sketched a pretty

flower and then turned it into a fluffy pom-

pom. She was so busy drawing and colouring in

that she nearly didn't hear their class teacher,

Miss Davey, tell them she had an important

announcement to make. **Whoops!**

Hello Kitty put her pencil down and glanced

quickly across the table. Her friends Fifi, Tammy

and Dear Daniel were all looking expectantly at

Miss Davey. Hello Kitty smiled – these were her

best friends. Such great friends in fact that they had started a club, and together the four of them made up the Friendship Club! They met up all the time to do loads of fun things like crafting and baking and having fashion makeovers.

Miss Davey waited until she had the whole class's attention and everyone was completely

silent before she started to speak. She began

by telling them all that there were only three

days left till half-term holidays, but Hello Kitty

and the class already knew that, *of course!*

They all knew what they were going to do

in the holidays. Dear Daniel was going away

travelling with his dad, but

the rest of the Friendship

Club were spending

the break at home. They had already made plans for lots of fun things to do together – like sleepovers, makeovers, and trips out – and Hello Kitty couldn't wait! Just then, Miss Davey made her big announcement. The teachers had decided that there was going to be a cross-country race on Friday to finish off the term

with a bang, followed by a family picnic! How **SUPER** was that! She asked people to put their hands up if they wanted to enter the race.

Hello Kitty *and friends*

Excited chatter filled the air. Hello Kitty put up her hand, but Dear Daniel already had his hand up in the air and Fifi was quick to join him. Hello Kitty wasn't surprised. Fifi was really

sporty – although ice-skating was her favourite sport, she was good at running too. As for Dear Daniel, he just **l♥ved** doing anything outdoors. Tammy liked sports too, but she hesitated and looked at Hello Kitty, and didn't put her hand up.

Miss Davey was still talking to the class; explaining how the race would work. It was going to take place in the big town park and would start by the swings and slides, and then they would run through the woods until they came out alongside the lake. There would then be a straight sprint to the finish by

the picnic area. It was going to be quite

a **long** race!

Hello Kitty nudged Tammy and smiled but

Tammy bit her lip and shook her head. She

didn't want to go in such a long race.

Hello Kitty put her hand down and thought hard. She didn't want Tammy to miss out on such a fun event! Looking around, her eyes fell on the pom-pom she had drawn and suddenly she had one of her **special, super, Hello Kitty ideas!**

They didn't have to actually run in the race to take part, did they? They could do something else

instead. Maybe she and Tammy could organise a cheerleading team!

Excitement rushed through Hello Kitty. There would be costumes to make and dance routines to think up. It would be so much fun! She quickly whispered her plan to Tammy.

Tammy beamed. What a brilliant idea! But what would Miss Davey think?

Hello Kitty shot her hand up in the air again and waved to get her teacher's attention. Miss Davey **smiled** and asked her to wait a moment while she finished writing down all the runners' names, and then she turned to Hello Kitty. Hello Kitty sat up straight in her seat and explained her idea.

Miss Davey looked thoughtful for a moment, and then she grinned. It wasn't just a good idea...

it was a great idea! Hello Kitty grinned straight back. Not just a great idea but a whole lot of fun, too!

Making Plans

The very next day, the Friendship Club got to work. Fifi and Dear Daniel were going for a run after school to practice for the race, but they said that they would meet at Hello Kitty's house when they had finished. The whole Friendship

Hello Kitty *and friends*

Club was allowed to stay for dinner too, so
they'd be able to get **lots** of things done!
Hello Kitty and Tammy linked arms and made
their way over to the school gates where Mama
White was waiting to drive them home. Hello

Kitty waved goodbye to her
twin sister, Mimmy. Mimmy
was staying on for flute
practice with her best
friend, Alice, so she
wasn't coming home with
them just then.

It didn't take long for
Mama White to drive home. Hello Kitty and
Tammy *jumped* out of the car, burst
through the front door and ran straight through
to the living room and put on a cheerleading
DVD that Hello Kitty had got for her birthday.
They wanted to get started! They had decided

they needed to practise some cheerleading

moves before they could put together an actual

routine. Concentrating hard, the two friends

worked their way through a star **jump**, a high

'V', where they put their arms above their head

and a low, upside down 'V' where they put their

hands down by their sides. There was a lot of

clapping, as well as practising different shapes,

like the T-shape with their arms straight out

from their sides, and another one where they

pumped their arms up into fists. The DVD

got a lot more complicated after that with lots

of different cheerleaders performing the same moves but on different beats of the music! **Whew!** Hello Kitty and Tammy agreed that they could work on that later; they would just try out the easy stuff for now. Tammy looked thoughtful. She looked at Hello Kitty, and asked what music she thought they would dance to? Hello Kitty pulled out her music player and scrolled through to her favourite band – the **Fizzy Pops!** They were the best! She put on one of her favourite songs, *Falling Star*, and then she and Tammy stood in

front of the big living room mirror and started

to put all the moves they had learned together

into a real routine – first a high 'V', clap, then

a low 'V', clap. They spun and twirled, jumping

into a T-shape and then breaking the motion by

pumping their arms in the next position. Now

they bent and touched down to the ground

and back up again, finishing off with a big star

jump into the air.

Phew! It was thirsty work!
Luckily, just then Mama came
in with some lemonade and
fruity flapjacks. Yummy!
They ate their snack and
started practising again,
adding in some more steps
between the jumps. They were
going to have to practise doing their routine
holding pom-poms too!

Hello Kitty grabbed a couple of cushions
from the sofa and handed them to Tammy.
They didn't exactly look like pom-poms, but
they would have to do for now!

Tammy giggled as Hello Kitty led the way. They jumped back into a 'V', marched three steps forward, then three steps back, and then they twisted to the right, waving the cushions in the air.

At first, the two girls found it **hard** to keep their moves in time to the music, and to each other! When Hello Kitty turned one way, Tammy turned the other. The next thing they knew, they were in a tangle on the floor. They looked at each other and burst out laughing.

OK, so that wasn't quite right, but it was a start
and they were having a lot of fun!

One… two… one… two…

they tried again.

At that moment, Mama
came back in. She wanted
to know how they were
getting on. Hello Kitty told
her that they had almost
got one routine worked out.
Would Mama please watch

and tell them what she thought, she asked?

Mama settled down into the big armchair
as the girls started their routine. They spun

and clapped, and at the end Mama gave them

a big round of applause. She thought it was

wonderful! Hello Kitty wasn't sure though. It

had been OK, but something was bothering her.

What was still missing from their routine?

At that moment, the doorbell rang and Mama

got up to answer it. It was Mimmy; Alice's

mother had dropped her back. Mimmy watched

the routine as they had a second practice. Then

she asked if she could join in. Of **course**

she could!

Hello Kitty and Tammy quickly taught

Mimmy the moves and then they ran through

the routine again. Seeing Mimmy beside

Tammy made Hello Kitty realise exactly what it was that had been bothering her. The whole cheerleading routine was so much better when Mimmy was in it too – they needed more **people!** Maybe they could persuade Fifi and Dear Daniel to do it with them instead of running the race?

Mama gently pointed out that it wouldn't be very fair to ask them not to run the race, as they loved running and were practising hard. Surely there must be other people at school who didn't like running in races, she suggested, and who would join in with Hello Kitty and Tammy? Cheerleading was so much fun! Mama thought hard. Why didn't they put up a poster to try and get some more people that way, she said?

Hello Kitty and Tammy smiled. They thought that was a great idea! At that moment, the

doorbell rang, and Mimmy ran to open it. It was

Dear Daniel and Fifi, just in time to help design

the poster. Mama said she would leave them all

to it while she cooked dinner.

Hello Kitty went to the cupboard and pulled

out her box of crafting materials. In it was

all the stuff they needed to make their poster

totally **brilliant!**

Starry stickers

Glue

Scissors

Glitter pens

If Fifi and Dear Daniel didn't mind working on

the poster, Hello Kitty and Tammy could make

some *real* pom-poms to replace the cushions

they had been practising with.

Hello Kitty started pulling out crepe paper.

There were so many colours to choose from

– bright pink, orange, yellow… Eventually they

settled on orange. Hello Kitty put a batch of sheets together, and then she started to fold it backwards and forwards into folds, like on a concertina, straightening out each layer with a ruler. When she had finished, she folded it in half and Tammy tied a piece of string around the middle. They snipped the top of each end off at a slant and started to pull each layer back into puffs.

Ta da! After a while, Tammy proudly held up a perfectly formed, round orange pom-pom.

Fifi and Dear Daniel clapped. Tammy smiled, and then set to work making some more while Hello Kitty made a start on designing the rest of their cheerleading costumes. At last, it was nearly dinner time. Before they all went through to the kitchen they showed Mama what they had been doing. Mama **l♥ved** the poster and the pom-poms. Hello Kitty held

up the costume designs — she had decided on

little yellow skirts and orange tops, with bows

to match their pom-poms. Mama thought the

designs were SUPER! Hello Kitty hoped they

would be the *perfect* outfits to cheer

on her friends. And not just to cheer on her

friends — Mama White reminded them all that

there was going to be a mum and dad race too, and that she and Papa White were going to enter! She looked a bit worried about it. She wasn't all that good at running, so she hoped she wouldn't let the side down...

Hello Kitty gave her mum a **big hug.**

She could never let the side down and besides, wasn't Mama always telling her that it was the taking part and not the winning that mattered?

Mama gave her daughter a big squeeze, too and nodded. Hello Kitty beamed. There was so much to organise, but it was going to be so much fun. **Hooray!**

New Recruits

Later that week, Hello Kitty and Tammy

stood back from the school notice board and

looked at the poster they had just pinned up.

As soon as Hello Kitty had got into school that

morning she had found Mrs Brown the head

teacher, and asked her permission to put it
up. When Mrs Brown had heard it was for a
cheerleading team to support the runners in the
race, she had been **very happy** to agree!

Hello Kitty looked
at Tammy. What did
she think? Tammy
said the poster looked
amazing. It was right
in the middle of the
board and had little
silver stars all round
it and pictures of pom-poms across the top,
as well as a section for people to write their

names in if they wanted to sign up.
Dear Daniel and Fifi had done
a brilliant job! Tammy was
sure that by break time that
morning they would have
loads of people signed up to
join the cheerleading team.

Hello Kitty linked arms with her friend and
they made their way to class. It was two of
their *favourite* lessons before lunch that
morning – Science and Nature followed by
Art – but all that Hello Kitty could think about
was getting back to the poster and seeing how
many people had written their names down.

Hello Kitty *and friends*

Her tummy **fizzed** with excitement as she sat through the Science and Nature lesson. Just before break, Miss Davey noticed Hello Kitty and Tammy looking at the clock and smiled. She said that if they put away their pen pots, they could go off five minutes early to see the poster!

Hello Kitty and Tammy cleared up, then quickly scraped back their chairs and dashed

down the corridor. They stopped in front of the notice board. Hello Kitty stared. What? **Oh no!** Not one person had signed up! Not a single person had added their name!

Tammy wondered aloud if it was because they hadn't waited long enough. It was only break time, remember… Everyone would have been in class all morning. But Hello Kitty pointed out that the whole school would have had to pass the notice board on their way to their classrooms. Perhaps… they just didn't want to be cheerleaders?

They both felt a bit sad for a moment but
then Hello Kitty took a deep breath. They
wouldn't give up! She thought hard, and an idea
popped into her head. Why didn't they see if

they could do a mini-routine at lunchtime, in
front of everyone? Then the whole school would

all see how much *fun* it was and people might sign up!

Tammy agreed, but then she remembered that they didn't have any of the outfits made up yet, and they didn't even have their pom-poms, which they had left at Hello Kitty's house. **How** could they make a routine look good? Hello Kitty looked thoughtful. Maybe they should ask Miss Davey for help...

Miss Davey listened patiently when the two girls appeared back at the classroom and explained what had happened. They told her about their idea for putting on a mini-routine.

Miss Davey thought it was a *very* good plan.

She suggested that for outfits, Hello Kitty and

Tammy could borrow two of the school netball

team's skirts from the PE teacher, and said she

would let them use some crepe paper from the

art cupboard to make pom-poms. They could

do that in their Art lesson after break time –

everyone would be working on things like flags

and banners for the cross-country race anyway.

If they worked hard, they should be ready in

time for the lunch break.

Hello Kitty and Tammy hugged Miss Davey.

She really was the best teacher ever!

Quickly, they set to work. The PE teacher lent them two netball skirts, and then in the Art lesson they made two pom-poms each and found some orange ribbon to tie in their hair. When they were ready, Miss Davey let them have a practice in the hall. Hello Kitty and Tammy ran through the whole routine. They couldn't **wait** to put on the show!

At lunchtime, everyone gathered round. Fifi
and Dear Daniel came to support them too and
were right at the front of the crowd.

Hello Kitty and Tammy jumped and high-fived
their way through their routine. They swung
their pom-poms and danced through their steps.

LET ME HEAR YOU YELL GO!

LET ME HEAR YOU YELL RUN!

LET ME HEAR YOU YELL WIN!

LET ME HEAR YOU YELL, GO RUN WIN!

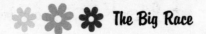

They spun and leaped and the routine finished to the sound of loud applause. Hello Kitty and Tammy were breathless but **happy!** Before they even had time to grab a pen and paper, everyone had flocked around them to sign up. Hello Kitty looked across at Tammy and smiled. Maybe things were going to be all right after all!

Cheerleaders!

At lunch the next day Hello Kitty and Tammy

stood in the school playground, holding a plate

of biscuits and a pile of pom-poms. They felt

a little bit nervous. Ten people had signed up

yesterday, including Mimmy, but what if they

didn't all show up for the practice? Hello Kitty

jumped anxiously from one foot to the other.

Hello Kitty and Tammy needn't have worried!

In no time at all, they were ***surrounded***

by the ten volunteers. Mimmy and her friend

Alice were the first to appear. They were joined

by some other girls from class 3B, a girl and a

boy from the year below and three older girls

from the year above them. The last person was Tammy's twin brother, Timmy! **Hooray!** Now that everyone had arrived, Hello Kitty started by organising them all into three groups of four. She was going to take one of the groups, while Tammy was going to teach the second group and Mimmy and Alice, who already knew the routine from the other day, were going to help the third. When they had perfected their routine in each individual group, they would join up.

Hello Kitty started off by showing her team how to do a high 'V' and a low 'V'. Then they

learnt the 'T' and the fist pumps, and how to do a perfect star jump. Now they just had to do all of it together with pompoms! Hello Kitty handed them out. Soon, her group knew the routine perfectly and Hello Kitty left them practising.

She walked over to watch the other groups. They seemed to have got it all sorted out too! Hello Kitty called out and the three groups came together. Soon they were **bobbing** and **diving** and flicking their pom-poms.

It was perfect! All that was left was the grand finale where Hello Kitty would lead them all out, with her standing at the head of a 'V' shape, and they would kick their legs up in perfect unison. Hello Kitty felt a warm happy **glow** flood through her as she watched everyone working so hard and doing the routine that she and Tammy had made up. Finally, when they had practised and practised until they could do no more, Hello Kitty called out for them to stop. It was time for a break! They munched happily on

the biscuits Hello Kitty had made and enjoyed the sun. Looking at everyone laughing and chatting, Hello Kitty didn't think she could have felt better. Everyone agreed that they would all meet again the next morning – the day of the actual race – for one final practice, before they did the routine in front of **everyone!**

She turned to Tammy and smiled. So far, so good!

After school, Hello Kitty and Tammy went to watch Dear Daniel and Fifi practising their running in the park with some of the other children from school. Fifi and Dear Daniel were right up at the front of the group of runners speeding around the park. Hello Kitty and Tammy clapped as they watched from the side. Their friends were good – *really good!* There was just one more lap of the park to go before they entered into the trees. Fifi's hair

was escaping from her ponytail as she ran. Dear Daniel was a bit **red** in the face, but he was keeping up with everyone just fine.

Hello Kitty gave a little skip of excitement as she thought of how their cheerleading would encourage her friends the next day. Maybe the cheering would even help them to win! She

had lost sight of them now as they ran into the

trees, and not a moment too soon... As it was

beginning to spit with rain! Hello Kitty held

out her hands. She hadn't brought an umbrella

because it had been such good weather all

week. **Oh dear!** She hoped that it

wasn't going to rain tomorrow for the big race.

She turned to Tammy, who was also looking up at the clouds, and suggested that they make a run for it before it really started to pelt down. Tammy agreed. Soon, they were back at Hello Kitty's house, all dry and warm.

That evening as Hello Kitty snuggled down in her bed, she couldn't stop thinking about the next day. She could see it all already – the runners charging along, the cheerleaders performing an *amazing* routine, encouraging all the runners on. Everyone would be clapping. Now there she was, smiling, as Miss

Hello Kitty *and friends*

Davey told everyone how The Friendship Club

had organised it all. Before she knew it, Hello

Kitty had fallen fast asleep....

The Big Race

The next morning, Hello Kitty woke up early.

Did she dare look out and see what the weather

was like? Was it raining? She opened one eye a

little, and then the other. She could just see the

first few rays of sun sneaking their way through

Hello Kitty *and friends*

the crack in her curtains. **Hooray!** It was going to be a lovely day! Hello Kitty rushed down the stairs and into the kitchen.

Mimmy was already there, munching her way
through a bowl of cereal while Mama White
prepared the picnic for the whole family's lunch.
Hello Kitty was so *excited* that she wasn't
very hungry, but Mama asked her to sit down
and eat something. After all, she would need
lots of energy for her cheerleading routines!

Papa came into the kitchen then, to collect the picnic and load up the car. Hello Kitty finished her breakfast and *ran* to grab the pom-poms – she mustn't forget those! Soon, they were all packed up and on their way.

The park was a hive of activity as Papa drove up. A group of people were already marking out the cross-country race with cones and ribbons while another group laid out a table of silver cups as prizes. There was a row of bunting to mark the start and the finish of the race and some teachers were calling out instructions over a handheld loudspeaker. A **long** queue of runners were already standing in front of a

table to collect numbers to put on their backs,

so everyone would know who was who while

they were running.

Hello Kitty looked across the

field. **Lots** of families had

come to watch – there was

Dear Daniel with his mother

and father, and Fifi with her

parents and little brother and

sister. Tammy was with her twin

brother, Timmy, and their parents. Everyone

was laying out their

picnic rugs and

choosing their

spots for the day – some in the shade, some in the sun. Hello Kitty had agreed to meet the rest of the cheerleaders under the big oak, close to the start, to have one last run-through of their routines. She ran over with the pom-poms.

Everyone had come already changed into their costumes. It was still a little squelchy underfoot from the rain the day before but the sun was already starting to dry out the muddy puddles and none of the cheerleaders let the wet grass worry them. Hello Kitty led the first cheer.

All of the cheerleaders cried out in unison.

Fifi looked over from where she was standing

with the other runners, all trying to get the best

position at the starting line, and **grinned.**

Hello Kitty and the rest of the cheerleaders

hurried over to a point at the end of the first stretch of the course, where they would perform the first part of their routine.

One… Two… Three... Bang! The starting gun went and the runners set off. It was a good start for both Fifi and Dear Daniel – they were in the middle of the pack. The cheerleaders started singing and spinning. Hello Kitty bobbed down into a bend and back up into a high 'V', before **jumping** into a star.

She looked around her. Everyone was keeping in perfect time!

She glanced at the runners. Dear Daniel and
Fifi were both **still** around the middle of the
pack but they had crept up to the front a bit.

The first runners headed into the trees.

Hello Kitty realised the cheerleading team
should move so that they would be near the end
of the race to cheer people over the finish line.
She called to everyone to gather up their stuff
and make their way over to the
other side of the park. They

quickly got into position and waited for the

runners to come out of the trees. And soon...

Here they were! Hello Kitty gave everyone the

signal for them all to start up again. As they

started their next routine, she saw Fifi at the

front of the pack. *Hooray!* But

where was Dear Daniel?

Hello Kitty felt a rush of relief as she saw him sprinting out of the trees. The runners were travelling fast now – all closing in on each other. But Dear Daniel was quick. He was coming up the outside, slowly taking on each of the other runners, one by one. Now he was in fifth place... now in fourth. Hello Kitty cheered.

Come on Dear Daniel!

What happened next took Hello Kitty completely by surprise. It all seemed to happen

in slow motion, like watching it in a movie.
Before Hello Kitty could call his name again,
Dear Daniel had *slipped* in a puddle. The
others were all running so fast that they were
past him in a flash.

Hello Kitty's heart was in her mouth. Would Dear Daniel get up and run again? She looked at the cheerleaders. It was almost time for her to lead them out into the 'V' for their grand finale! But what about Dear Daniel? He was slowly getting to his feet. He looked very unhappy. Hello Kitty felt a lump rising in her throat. Dear Daniel was one of her oldest friends. She **had** to go over to him!

Calling out to Tammy and without a second thought, Hello Kitty left the cheerleaders and rushed across the park to help.

Dear Daniel stumbled to his feet just as Hello Kitty got there. She saw the disappointment on his face as he stood up, but he tried to **smile** when he saw her. He told Hello Kitty he wanted to finish the race.

Of course he did, Hello Kitty declared –
and she would run beside him, *every* step
of the way!

Dear Daniel's knees were all muddy and
bruised, but he started to run with Hello Kitty
at his side. Step by step, they headed towards

the finish line. They weren't quite at the back
of the race as the last few runners were still on
their way in behind them. Hello
Kitty glanced over to the
cheerleaders and was
really pleased to see
that Tammy had taken
charge and was leading them

out into the big 'V' for the end of their routine.
She wasn't able to lead her team in their final
cheer, but she knew that helping Dear Daniel
was **far more** important!

There were just fifty metres left to go of
the race.

Hello Kitty *and friends*

Hello Kitty and Dear Daniel made a last dash together and that was it... They were over the finish line!

Dear Daniel's parents hurried over to check he was all right, followed by Fifi, and then Tammy came *running* over with the other cheerleaders too. They all said how brave he was to finish the race.

Dear Daniel smiled and remarked that he would never have finished the race without

Hello Kitty's help! She was such a good friend.

Hello Kitty **blushed.** She'd been glad

to help even though it had meant leaving the

cheerleading team.

The Friendship Club all hugged and Fifi

announced that what Hello Kitty had done had

made her think of a new rule for the Friendship

Club. It should be:

A good friend
is always there
to help you
when you fall.

Hello Kitty beamed. There was only one

word for that rule... SUPER!

Perfect Prizes

The Friendship Club set about enjoying the rest of the day. The teachers and parents had set up lots of other stalls, like a lucky dip and apple-bobbing, a cake stall and a bouncy castle. As the four friends walked around the park,

eating ice creams and laughing with each other,

they couldn't have been any **happier!**

When it came to the mum and dad race, they

all lined up to watch.

Mama White, much to everyone's surprise,

won the mums' race, whilst Tammy and

Timmy's dad took first place in the dads! Papa White was right towards the back, but he didn't mind. Running really wasn't his thing!

Hello Kitty grinned at him, and **giggled.** She had a cheerleading costume she could lend him if he wanted, she called out! Everyone laughed.

All too soon, the events of the day were over and it was time for the prize- giving. They all gathered around the table where Mrs Brown stood in front of the array of shiny cups,

waiting to present the prizes. The results of the main event – the cross-country race – were announced in reverse order. A boy called Jack had come in third and went up to collect his yellow rosette. Fifi was over the moon to collect her bright blue second-place rosette, and a boy and a girl from another class had come in joint first! It had been *too close* to split them!

They happily held the cup up between them, each holding one of the silver arms.

Mrs Brown made a special mention of Dear Daniel and explained how if he hadn't slipped, he would have been up there with them too. Everyone gave a **loud** cheer. Then Tammy and Timmy's dad was called up to collect his cup for the dads' race and Mama White went up to collect her first prize too.

There was just one cup left standing on the table. But who was that for? The prizes for all of the events had been handed out hadn't they?

Mrs Brown cleared her throat. This silver cup was a particularly *special* one, she explained, because it wasn't for the person who had run the fastest or the longest. It wasn't even for the person who had worked the hardest. This was a very important cup indeed, as it was for the person who was the best sport. She was proud to announce that the person who had won the cup had been the best sport of the day by putting her friend above herself. And that person was…

Hello Kitty!

For a moment, Hello Kitty couldn't **believe** it. She didn't move. But then her friends pushed her forward.

Dear Daniel whispered to her that he had told Mrs Brown how she had given up her role at the front of the cheerleading team to help him.

As she held the trophy above her head and everyone clapped and cheered, Hello Kitty felt **very** proud.

She looked across at her family and friends — to where Dear Daniel stood with Tammy and Fifi, and then over to where her sister Mimmy

Hello Kitty and friends

was standing with Mama and Papa, and smiled

the biggest smile she could.

She didn't think she had ever felt happier...
Hooray!

The end

Turn over the page for activities and
fun things that you can do with your
friends – just like Hello Kitty!

Hold your own sports day!

Hello Kitty and her friends love being sporty – especially when they can do it together! It's easy to put together your own fun sports day, and compete against your friends. Follow the instructions on these pages, and get ready for some sporty fun!

Instructions

Firstly, you'll need an outdoor area with lots of room, like a park or school ground! You'll also need a grown-up to supervise you and decide the winners, and to help you mark out a start and finishing line for the races and boundaries for the games.

For the races and games, you will also need:

- Ribbon, string or scarves
- Balloons; at least one per person (and some spares!)
- Spoons; one per person

Three-legged race 4+ people

1. Each racer needs to pick a partner, stand next to each other and tie your inside legs together at the ankle and just under the knee.

2. Put your arms around each other, and you're ready to race! The winner is the first pair to the finish line.

HELLO KITTY TIP

These races aren't won by the fastest runner!

Balloon Relay 4+ people

1. Divide into two teams. Each team spaces their members evenly between the start and finish lines, with the first runner at the starting line holding a balloon.

2. On 'GO!' the first runner puts the balloon between their knees, and runs to the next runner.

3. Runner one passes it from their knees to Runner two's knees, and repeat until the last runner makes it to the end with the balloon!

4. If you drop the balloon on the way, you have to go back to where you started!

Balloon Tennis 2-4 people

1. Tie a piece of string across the middle of your 'court' as a net, and mark out the edges too.

2. Players stand on each side of the net, and take it in turns to serve the balloon to each other!

3. The balloon must go over the net each time, and not touch the ground at all. If it does, the other player gets a point!

4. The winner is the first player to ten points.

Spoons and balloons! 2+ people

1. Each runner lines up at the start with a balloon balanced on their spoon, held out in front of them.

2. The winner is the person who makes it to the end with the balloon on their spoon! No holding it on allowed, and if you drop it, you have to pick it up and put it back on!

You can have lots more races and games at your sports day – just use your imagination to come up with some more!

Make your medals!

What do you give a winner? A medal of course!
Follow the instructions below to make your
own shiny medals to give to your friends.

MAKE SURE YOU ASK MAMA OR PAPA TO HELP!

You will need:

- Metallic cardboard (in gold, silver and bronze, or just one colour).
- Scissors
- Ribbon
- A blunt pencil

MEDAL
TEMPLATE

What to do

1. Copy or trace the template shown on to your metallic cardboard, and cut it out. Cut out the small hole in the top too. Don't forget to ask a grown-up for help when you're using scissors!

2. Use your blunt pencil to draw a design on the back of it. You will need to write backwards so that when you turn it over, the letters are the right way round! Try a big **1** for the winner!

3. Go over your design with your blunt pencil, pushing down hard. This will push your design right through to the other side.

4. Turn over your medal to see your design on the front. Thread some ribbon through (enough so the medal can hang around your neck), and tie the ends together.

Ta da!

You've got medals fit for champions... You can give gold to first place, silver to second place and bronze to third place – or the same colour to everyone!

Hello Kitty Tip

Everyone on your sports day is a winner.

Why not give medals to other categories too?

Take a look at Hello Kitty's list:

- *The Best Sport*
- *Tried the Hardest*
- *Cheered the Loudest!*

Turn the page for a sneak peek at

and friends'

next adventure...

The Makeover Party

Hello Kitty let out a little sigh and fanned herself under the shade of the tree. It was SO hot today! She looked across her garden to where her two friends Fifi and Tammy, were jumping in and out of the water sprinkler and spraying each other. They were having so much fun. It was time to join them!

It wasn't quite Waterworld, where they

had been meant to be going that day, but with their other friend Dear Daniel away on a trip with his dad, that would just have to wait. They couldn't possibly go without him!

Hello Kitty jumped up and raced over to join her friends. She was wearing a pink-and-white polka-dotted swimsuit, a big floppy pink hat and her favourite matching pink flip-flops. She quickly kicked off her flip-flops, spun her hat across the grass, and ran through the spray too, giggling. It was just so much fun! Super!

Hello Kitty looked around her. The recent rain and the hot summer sun had sent the garden into full bloom and flowers of all sizes and colours were lining the flower beds. The air was filled with a lovely sweet smell from all the beautiful blossom. Hmmm… It all gave her a really great idea, but only if Fifi and Tammy wanted to do it too!

Hello Kitty looked across at them. Along with Dear Daniel they were her best friends in the whole world. Together, they made up the Friendship Club – a club that met after school and in the holidays to do all sorts of fun things like crafting and baking and dancing and going on trips. They even had a friendship manual where they added rules about friendship as they went along!

Hello Kitty called out to Tammy and Fifi

and told them her idea. How about they spent the rest of the day making their very own homemade perfumes, she suggested? It was getting really warm so it would be good to do something inside out of the heat, and there were plenty of petals to choose from in the garden.

Fifi and Tammy both clapped their hands in excitement and jumped up and down. They thought it was a brilliant idea! They loved things like making perfumes and with Dear Daniel not back for two more days, it seemed like perfect timing. Dear Daniel wasn't quite as keen on flowery, girly things as they were – in fact, said Fifi, if he was here, they would probably be playing football! Hello Kitty and Tammy giggled.

Hello Kitty thought hard, and told the other girls that she even had a collection of little glass bottles in her bedroom which they could put the perfumes in. Perfect!

Tammy thought she would like to make a rose perfume. Yummy; rose was her favourite scent.

Fifi thought she would like something a little more fruity...what about rosemary and lemon? She could get some rosemary from Papa White's herb garden, and Hello Kitty's mama would be sure to have a lemon inside!

Which just left Hello Kitty to decide which

perfume she wanted to make. She thought hard and looked all around her. Big clumps of bushes with purple flowers and silvery leaves were growing all around the garden. Lavender! Now that would be just perfect...

Find out what happens next in...

Hello Kitty
and friends

The Makeover Party
·A HELLO KITTY ADVENTURE·

Hello Kitty
and friends

The TV Star
A HELLO KITTY ADVENTURE

Hello Kitty
and friends

The Big Race
A HELLO KITTY ADVENTURE

Collect all of the Hello Kitty and Friends Stories!

HELLO KITTY
The Friendship Club

HELLO KITTY
and friends
The School Trip

·A HELLO KITTY STORY·
HELLO KITTY
and friends
The Summer Fair

HELLO KITTY
and friends
The Pop Princess

·A HELLO KITTY STORY·
HELLO KITTY
and friends
The Wedding Day

A HELLO KITTY STORY
HELLO KITTY
and friends
The Beach Holiday

·A HELLO KITTY STORY·
HELLO KITTY
and friends
The Treasure Hunt

A HELLO KITTY STORY
HELLO KITTY
and friends
The Talent Show

·A HELLO KITTY CHRISTMAS SPECIAL·
HELLO KITTY
and friends
The Christmas Present
TWO SPECIAL CHRISTMAS STORIES

Christmas Special: Two Stories in One!